DRAGONSLAYER™

The Storybook Based on the Movie

Random House 🏠 New York

Paramount Pictures Corporation and Walt Disney Productions
Present
A Barwood-Robbins Production
DRAGONSLAYER™
Executive Producer Howard W. Koch
Written by Hal Barwood & Matthew Robbins
Produced by Hal Barwood
Directed by Matthew Robbins
Storybook adaptation by Larry Weinberg

Library of Congress Cataloging in Publication Data: Weinberg, Larry. Dragonslayer : the storybook based on the movie. (Movie storybooks) SUMMARY: As a dragon is decimating the young female population of a kingdom, the villagers come to the last of the great magicians for help. [1. Magic—Fiction. 2. Dragons—Fiction.] I. Dragonslayer. [Motion Picture] II. Title. III. Series. PZ7.W4362Dr [Fic] 80-29524 AACR1 ISBN: 0-394-84849-7 (trade); 0-394-94849-1 (lib. bdg.) Manufactured in the United States of America   1   2   3   4   5   6   7   8   9   0

TM designates trademark of Paramount Pictures Corporation

Book printed by Random House, Inc., under exclusive license from Paramount Pictures Corporation, the trademark owner.

 is a trademark of Paramount Pictures Corporation

Galen
Ulrich's eager
young apprentice

Valerian
A brave Urlander
who seeks Ulrich's help

Vermithrax
The monstrous dragon that
brings death and destruction
to the people of Urland

Simon
The clever blacksmith
who is Valerian's father

Ulrich
Last of the world's
great magicians

Hodge
The magician's loyal,
cantankerous old servant

The King of Urland
The deceitful ruler
of a troubled land

Elspeth
A beautiful,
strong-willed princess

Tyrian
A cruel knight
who serves the king

High on a hill stood a crumbling castle. Inside it, among the cobwebs, lived an old man. Once his powers had been great. But now they were slowly leaving him. And yet his name still rang out through all the kingdoms of the world. For he was Ulrich, the Wizard of Cragganmore, last of the great magicians.

This pitch-black night he stood alone in his tower. Before him was a bowl made of stone. It seemed like any other bowl. Ordinary, too, was the water he poured into it. But now he passed a hand over the bowl and spoke.

> *"Spirit of water,*
> *Sleeping still,*
> *Awake! and hear*
> *Thy master's will!"*

Slowly, the dark water began to glow. Bending low, the magician commanded the bowl to show him the secrets of the night.

At Ulrich's words, the water in the bowl began to move in a circle —slowly, at first, then faster and faster.

The sorcerer gazed deeply into the whirlpool within the bowl. Soon the shape of a cave formed in its watery depths. Smoke was rising from it as if it were coming from the very bottom of the earth. In front of the cave stood a wooden post hung with iron chains. Shreds of dried flesh and pieces of burned cloth hung from the chains.

The magician passed his hand over the bowl once more.

> *"Go back in time*
> *For I must see*
> *That which caused*
> *This thing to be!"*

As the magician commanded, so it was done. The flesh became a young maiden. And the cloth became her dress. Soldiers were tying her to the post.

"Spare me! Oh spare me!" cried the voice from within the bowl. "I am only sixteen! I don't want to die!"

The smoke from the cave grew thicker. It clouded the water in the bowl. From its murky depths came a horrible scream.

"What evil magic is this?" cried the wizard. "Bring back my vision!"

But the water in the bowl stayed dark. And now there was a pounding on the wizard's castle door. Visitors! Ulrich was about to leave the chamber of magic when the water in the bowl began to glow again. From deep within a voice whispered, "Ulrich! Stay and hear thy fate!"

The magician looked into the bowl once more. What he saw made his eyes open wide. "Vermithrax!" he whispered, his voice shaking.

Ulrich's old servant, Hodge, rose up from his bed and went out of his chamber. "Who dares come to this place at such an hour?" he muttered, as he went along the dark hallway.

Eight strangers stood at the great door holding lighted torches. The youngest spoke for all of them. "We come from Urland," he said. "We know it is late. But we have walked for many days. And we must speak to the magician."

"Go away!" said Hodge.

"But is this not the house of Ulrich?"

"Yes and no. Yes, it is. But no, he sees no one!"

"No one?"

"No one. Not even me."

"Please!"

"I've heard your pleas. Go home!" The door slammed in their faces.

"What now, Valerian?" exclaimed one of the men. "You have led us nowhere!"

"How quickly you give up, Greil," answered the young man. He raised his head and shouted at the castle windows. "Hear me, you who dwell in Cragganmore! Hear me, oh wizard in your tower! Yours is the power of magic. But ours is the power of waiting! We shall not leave till we are heard!"

Not a sound came back from the castle. Sadly, the travelers shook their heads. "He is deaf to us," said one of them.

But someone inside did hear them. He was young Galen, the magician's helper and apprentice. The boldness of the leader of the travelers impressed him. For there were not many who would call out like that to a sorcerer.

Galen left the window where he stood and climbed to the chamber of magic. Opening the heavy door, he gazed inside. There sat Ulrich, bent over his bowl of stone. He did not move. His eyes were fixed and staring as if he were dead—or in a trance.

"Master?" whispered Galen softly. "Can you hear me?"

The old man spoke, but his voice was strange. "I have seen it," he said.

"Seen what?" his helper asked quickly. But the sorcerer did not answer. "What have you seen?" Galen asked again.

"My death," said the magician. With a sweep of his arm, the old man sent the bowl crashing to the floor. "The visitors bring it."

"Then send them away!" cried Galen.

"No, no," said Ulrich. "They know nothing of it. They are peaceful and harmless." He slowly rose. "Tell Hodge to bid them enter," he ordered. "Go now, and I will follow."

Galen did as he was told. Soon the visitors were led into the dark hall of the great house. A moment later they beheld a flash of fire. Ulrich stood before them! The magician stretched forth his arm. "Light! Shine forth!" he commanded. At once, the room was filled with candlelight. "And heat!" The logs in the fireplace crackled into flames.

"Welcome," said Ulrich to his frightened guests. "And fear me not. I know who you are and why you have come. There is a great monster in your kingdom—a dragon whose breath is roaring fire. It lives underground in the darkest depths. But it has wings that can take it to the highest mountaintop. This beast has the power to shake the earth. Or burn a thousand villages to the ground." He smiled sadly at the Urlanders. "And you, of course, want me to slay him. I am flattered. But I am also very old. Tell me, why do you come to me?" His gaze fell on the youngest of them. "You who are named Valerian may speak."

Valerian stepped forward boldly. "It was a sorcerer's spell that made this dragon," he said. "And only another sorcerer can destroy it."

"Perhaps so and perhaps no," said the magician. "And perhaps I am the one that gave it life. Have you thought of that?"

"No! It was not you," answered Valerian. "You are known to be good."

"That may be," said the magician. "But I have never slain a dragon."

"There is no one else to turn to," said Valerian.

"No magicians in your own land?"

"None. All are dead. All the *real* ones."

"Ah yes," Urlich sighed. "It is the end of our time and the beginning of another. Perhaps that is just as well. What have we accomplished with all our magic? Is the world any better?" With a sigh, the wizard fell into his own thoughts.

Time passed. The travelers grew impatient. Then Ulrich spoke again. "I know your dragon," he said. "Its secret name is Vermithrax, and it is the greatest of all the serpents. Like myself, it is the last of its kind. One day, perhaps in your own lifetime, even Vermithrax will die."

"We cannot wait for that day," Valerian nearly shouted. "Our people live in constant fear of the dragon's anger! It is terrible to behold. It poisons our air with its stench. And we run in horror when it flies over our heads."

"It killed my daughter!" cried Greil.

"And mine!" sobbed another of the men. "They were sacrificed!"

Ulrich gazed at the two fathers. "Why were they allowed to die?" he asked.

"It could not be helped!" exclaimed Greil. "It was by the king's law! He has made a pact with the beast. Twice a year, at a lottery, one of our daughters is chosen for the dragon. In return, the dragon leaves the kingdom in peace."

"How are they chosen?" asked Galen.

Valerian answered him. "Every maiden's name is placed in a great box. Then one is picked by chance. She is taken that night to the dragon's cave —"

"Valerian!" Greil interrupted angrily. "Why do you say that every maiden's name goes in the box? It is only those of us who are poor who lose our children. The rich can buy their daughters' safety. They bribe the king's men. But the poor cannot. And the king makes very sure he does not risk the life of the princess!" He turned to Ulrich. "Great wizard! It is too late to help my own dear child. But, on bended knees, I beg you to save the children of the others."

The travelers waited for an answer, but Ulrich was silent. Galen looked into the old man's eyes.

There was something in them he had never seen before. Fear.

Galen, too, began to be afraid. Not for himself, but for his master.

"I must think," said Ulrich. And he left them.

The next morning, Galen walked with the magician in the garden. "Please!" he said. "Let me go in your place."

"That cannot be," answered the wizard. "You know so little. You make such foolish mistakes. You are not ready."

"Master," said the lad, "I was

not born for study. The more lessons I learn, the more I forget! There is only one hope for someone like me," he said, smiling. "It's to get out and *do* it! Just tell me how to get rid of the dragon—what spell to cast—and trust me! I already know how to stand the right way, and how to bring the forces together in my mind."

"You? How so? It may be that even my own powers cannot defeat the beast."

"Master, your wisdom is your strength. But *youth* is mine. The forces will obey me. Look! Do you see that bush?" Lifting his arms like a sorcerer, he tried to utter the words of power. "Light of light . . . " he began, and then broke off. "No, that's not it." He started again. "Power of power . . ."

Ulrich shook his head sadly.

"Oh yes! I remember now. *Both* are in it! Here we go—

Light of light,
Fire of fire,
Do thou bush
What I desire!"

Time passed, but nothing happened.

"What was the bush supposed to do?" the magician asked.

"Burn," said Galen, weakly.

"Oh really?" said Ulrich. He moved one hand just slightly. A lightning bolt flew out of the sky. A big rock next to the bush exploded. And the bush burst into flames. The force of the blow threw Galen to the ground. When he got up, bush and rock no longer existed. And the magician was gone.

ot long afterward, Ulrich came out of the castle with a pack on his old shoulders. He staggered under its weight as he joined the travelers from Urland.

He'll never be able to make the long journey to Urland, thought Galen. He is too old. His body is too weak. He will fall into a ditch somewhere and never get up! Galen fought back his tears. This is how the greatest man who ever lived will die!

"Don't fret so," the magician told his apprentice. "Good old Hodge will look after me. Meanwhile, Galen, you stay here. Work on your studies. We'll make a sorcerer of you yet!"

Ulrich signaled his servant to open the gate. And open it did— to a big surprise. Waiting there were three armed soldiers on horseback.

"Good morrow, all," said their leader, a knight named Tyrian. "You are a long way from your village, my friends," he said to the Urlanders. "And the king does not like his loving subjects to go too far. They might get into trouble."

"We've done nothing wrong," said Valerian.

"That remains to be seen," replied the knight. "We have a very contented dragon in our kingdom. That is how we'd like to keep it. We don't want to make our dragon angry, do we?"

The travelers said nothing. Tyrian turned to Ulrich.

"Our kingdom has no use for meddlers," he said. "Old fools who call themselves magicians should stay away from Urland."

Though Galen was unarmed, he started toward the knight. But Ulrich held him back.

"Do as I say," the wizard said quietly. "Go to my chamber and fetch the dagger from my iron box."

"Dagger?" asked Galen, alarmed.

"Did I hear 'dagger'?" Tyrian laughed scornfully. "Do you mean to harm me, old man?"

"Not at all," replied the wizard. "But I see that you desire a test of my powers." Ulrich turned to Gal-

en, who had not moved. He took a chain from around his neck and handed it to the youth.

"Take this amulet with you and put it away. Now go!"

Hurrying into the chamber, Galen tossed the amulet onto a table and looked around for the dagger. No sooner did he find the long, sharp, ivory-handled knife, than it went flying out of his hand. Before Galen could catch it, the dagger sailed out the window to the courtyard below, where Ulrich plucked it neatly out of the air.

Smiling, the wizard offered the

gleaming knife to the king's officer.

"They say you are good with a knife, Sir Tyrian. That you care not where you stick it, front or back. Then do me the kindness of thrusting this one deep into my heart." The sorcerer opened his robe so that his chest faced the point of the blade.

"No! No!"cried Galen. He rushed to the door of Ulrich's chamber. But magically, it slammed in his face.

Down below Tyrian held the dagger to the wizard's chest. He had killed many a man without a thought. But now, he had to try hard to keep his hand from shaking.

"What are you waiting for, brave soldier?" said Ulrich. "Do you fear an old fellow like me? Thrust it deep!"

With a sudden movement, the knight plunged the blade into the magician's body. The travelers gasped. No one moved. Time itself stood still. No blood came from the wound and, for a moment, Ulrich seemed unhurt. Then, without warning, the magician dropped to the ground. The great wizard of Cragganmore was dead.

"Stupid old fool!" cried Tyrian, as he mounted his horse. "You died believing in your own tricks!" He turned to the travelers. "Begone! I have done you a favor!" Then he rode off with all his men.

The door that held Galen prisoner now swung open. He raced outside and fell, weeping, beside his fallen master. He did not hear the sobbing words of the old servant, Hodge. "I must burn his body and gather the ashes. I must remember to throw the ashes in the lake of fire. Aye, that was his wish—his final wish."

That day, Valerian and the others helped Hodge and Galen start the funeral fire. As the flames climbed high, the travelers left Cragganmore and began their long journey home. Deep into the night the sparks of the fire flew into the sky like shooting stars. And, one by one, they went out.

Galen was overcome with grief. Now that his master was gone, Cragganmore was a joyless place. Everything in it reminded him of the old man he had cared about so deeply.

Sadly, Galen looked around the chamber of magic. His gaze fell upon the amulet he had thrown on the table the day before. It should be put away, he thought. He picked up the amulet and placed it carefully in Ulrich's old jewel box.

Then Galen started to clean up the master's chamber for the last time. Gathering a pile of books, he carried them to a trunk in the far corner of the room. As he lifted the lid, he stared in amazement at what lay inside. It was Ulrich's amulet.

How odd, he thought. Picking up the amulet, he placed it once again in the jewel box. But this time he made sure to close the box and lock it. Returning to his work, he carried some bottles to a cupboard to put them away. But when he opened the cupboard door— there was the amulet again!

For a moment, Galen panicked. He started to run out of the room— and bumped right into a glass jar that was floating in mid-air. Stuffed inside the narrow neck of the bottle was the amulet! Galen seized the jar and threw it to the ground. The instant it smashed, the amulet disappeared!

Now, though he looked everywhere, Galen could not find it. He dashed out of the chamber—and straight into Hodge.

"Hodge!" he shouted. "Help me find the master's amulet!"

"It's around your neck," said the servant.

Galen looked down. There it was. Amazed, he took it into his hands and stared at it.

"Be careful!" warned the old man. "They don't mix!"

"What don't?"

"Weak minds and strong magic!"

Galen looked again at the amulet. Suddenly he understood. It was a gift from Ulrich.

"He wanted me to have it!" said Galen with wonderment. "*I* am to slay the dragon!" He turned to the old servant. "Come with me, Hodge. It's time to leave here."

"What for?"

"There's work to do!"

"Well, you have your work and I have mine," was Hodge's mysterious reply.

Early the next day, the two set out through the forest. The kingdom of Urland was many leagues away. It was going to be a long, slow journey. And old Hodge was not making the trip any easier with his constant complaining.

"Oh, it's a sad, sad world in which we dwell," he muttered. "Doesn't matter who you are. You may be a king in your robes—or a beggar in your rags. But when

your time comes, no magic can
save you."

"Yes, I suppose so," said Galen.
He really wasn't listening. He'd
heard it all ten times before. His
mind was on something else — the
magic powers of the amulet. Toss-
ing a coin into the air, he silently
commanded it not to fall to the
ground. The coin remained in the
air.

"I did it!" he cried.

But old Hodge wasn't listening
to him either. "The kindest lord a
man could ask for," Hodge went
on. He started to cry. "I'm going
to miss him."

"So shall I," said Galen, as he
turned a leaf into a pear.

"No, you won't miss him,"
snapped Hodge. "You can't pull
any wool over these old eyes. All
you care about is tricks, and fool-
ishness. Well, mark my words.
It'll be a long walk before you fill
his shoes, and that's a fact."

Galen was beginning to think it was time to teach Hodge a lesson.

"Are you out of sorts, Hodge, because your pack is too heavy? Here—let me give you a hand with it." Galen pointed the amulet at Hodge. Magically, the old man's pack rose up and floated in the air beside him.

"Leave my pack alone!" cried Hodge, as he snatched it back angrily.

"Or perhaps the cold is bothering you," said Galen. "We can fix that easily enough." He raised the amulet again, his eyes gleaming with merriment.

"What cold? What are you talking about? Stop it!" shouted Hodge, as a huge fur coat the size of a bear fell over his shoulders.

Galen could hardly keep from laughing. "Or are you too hot? Is that what's making you cross?" Raising the amulet, he commanded "Begone!"

Instantly, the fur coat disappeared—and so did the rest of Hodge's clothing.

"Stop it! Stop it, I say!" shouted Hodge, in his underwear. "Have you no respect for the master's memory?"

"I've got as much respect as anyone," said Galen. "But you must remember, Hodge, *I* am the master now."

If you are the master, then the world is in trouble, thought Hodge. But now he knew better than to say it aloud.

It was the following night, and the travelers from Urland were gathered around an open fire. They were eating what little food they had been able to find in the woods. Everyone was miserable.

"We've worn ourselves out," said Greil. "And for what? A magician who couldn't keep himself alive, much less save anyone else. Ha! What a joke!"

"Greetings, travelers!" said a pleasant voice from the shadows.

"Who goes there?" shouted Valerian, jumping to his feet.

There was a puff of smoke and Galen appeared. "Behold!" he cried. "The Dragonslayer!"

"What is this idiot talking about?" shouted Greil. "Does he play games now with our misery?"

"No game," said Galen. "I am the new master sorcerer. I shall free you all from the dragon!"

"Is that so?" cried Greil. "Well, let us see if you are as useless as the last master sorcerer! This time let us try the point of *my* dagger!"

Half-crazed with anger, he drew his knife and charged at Galen. Valerian stepped in front of him nimbly, and swung a heavy branch at Greil's middle. With a grunt of pain, Greil dropped his knife and fell to the ground.

"I won't apologize for him," Valerian said to Galen. "But it was a year ago tonight that the soldiers gave his daughter to the dragon."

"It's unfair! So unfair!" Greil moaned. "She was only a child!" He burst into tears.

"I do hope that everyone is finished," said old Hodge, as he settled down by the fire. "Because the bones in my body are all saying, 'Hodge, why don't you settle down and go to sleep?'"

"Your bones give you pretty good advice," said Valerian. "Why don't we all take it?"

And so the travelers turned in for the night. They posted no guards, thinking there was no need for them. Had they known who was following, they would not have slept so peacefully.

Early the next morning, the travelers rose and started to gather up their packs. Galen noticed that Valerian was missing and went looking for him in the woods. Coming upon a stream, he found the young man's clothes lying on a rock. He heard a loud splash and saw Valerian swimming in the water.

For some reason, Valerian was not too happy to see Galen. He grew even unhappier when Galen decided to get undressed and join him.

"Don't come in!" he cried.

"Why not?" Galen asked.

"Because . . . because there are snapping turtles in the water!"

"Well, they don't seem to be snapping at you," said Galen. In he went and started swimming toward the other youth.

Valerian swam farther away. His face flushed with anger. "Fie! You are a lout!" he shouted. "Did I not say that I wish to be alone?"

"No, you did not say that you wish to be alone. But you may *be* alone! Just pretend you are somewhere else!" A beautiful stone glistened in the water near Valerian. Galen dove for it.

As soon as Galen was under water, Valerian rushed to the shore. Galen bobbed up just in time to see Valerian racing for a big rock.

"By the gods!" he exclaimed. "You're a *girl!*"

"Shout it louder!" she said, reaching for her clothes. "Then the whole world will know!"

"But why do you hide it?"

"Because they don't sacrifice *boys,* do they?"

"But the people in your village? Don't they . . . ?"

Valerian shook her head. "When I was born, my father told everyone that he had a son. He knew it was the only way to save me from the game of chance. But now I suppose you'll tell everyone."

"No one will find out from me!" Galen promised. "Can I come out of the water now?"

There was no answer. She was gone. Galen climbed out of the stream and got dressed. Bending over to take up his pack, he happened to touch the amulet hanging from his neck. Suddenly, the shape of a man on horseback appeared in the water. Tyrian!

Galen spun around to face the knight. But no one was behind him. Quickly, he turned back to look in the stream. The horse and rider were still there. "A vision!" exclaimed Galen.

In the vision Tyrian got down
from his horse. Slowly he reached
for an arrow and fitted it into his
long bow. Galen looked closer —
and saw the knight aiming his
drawn bow at Hodge.

Suddenly Galen was running.
His feet flew as he raced back to
the camp.

Breaking through a thicket,
Galen caught sight of the old man
up ahead. His warning cry and a
low whizzing sound came at the
same time. Hodge turned and fell
backward with an arrow sticking
out of his chest.

Galen rushed to the fallen old
man. "Hodge!" he cried.

"Galen? Can you hear me?"

The old man stared blankly up at the overhanging trees.

Galen bent closer. "I hear you."

"Tyrian shot me, but I can still talk. There's something that has to be done."

Galen nodded. "I know."

"Not the dragon! That's what Tyrian thought. The master's ashes! Throw them in the lake of fire!"

Galen peeled a small leather bag out of Hodge's clenched fist. "Master's ashes! Burning water!" gasped Hodge. "Find the lake, throw them in!"

Galen frowned at the leather bag. "Hodge—what does this mean?" But Hodge didn't hear the question.

"No," shouted Galen. "Not you! Don't you die too!" Tears rushed to his eyes. "Who is going to kick my bottom when I do something foolish? Or tell me stories of magic in the old days? Who will help me do our master's work?"

He bent down over the body. "Hodge? Listen to me. I'm a sorcerer now. I can do anything! I won't let you die!"

Galen pressed the amulet tightly and called upon the dreaded spirits of the dead to give up their newest victim. But the amulet turned red as fire in his palm. It burned into his flesh and he dropped it with a cry of pain.

The spirits had given their answer. And the old man remained as he had fallen.

As soon as Hodge was buried, the travelers set out again. They did not try to stop Galen from going along with them. But they were not pleased about it either. This mere boy who *called* himself a magician, they thought, might bring them trouble.

After many days' journey, the travelers reached a mist-covered lake. For two days and nights they rowed across it in a long boat. On the third day, at dawn, they reached Urland.

Now they made their way through a narrow mountain pass. Galen's eyes grew wide as he gazed about him. Wherever he looked, the trees were dead—burned and blackened. No living thing was in sight. Even the air seemed dead and still.

"What happened to this place?" asked Galen in wonderment.

"The work of the dragon," Valerian answered, as she hurried past him. "Move quickly. We are near the lair."

"Where is it?" Galen asked, his eyes roaming the rocky slopes. Before Valerian could answer, he spied a statue carved out of stone. It was in the shape of a dragon. Just beyond it was an opening in the mountainside—an entrance to the cave. Galen rushed toward it.

"Come back!" screamed Valerian, as she watched him climb. "Fool! Do you want to die?"

A moment later, Galen was stopped by a terrible sight. At the entrance of the cave stood a wooden post hung with iron chains. Bits of blackened cloth and bone were scattered on the ground nearby. Galen's breath caught in his throat.

This was the terrible place of sacrifice, where Greil and so many others had lost their young daughters forever! The young magician stared into the darkness of the cave, too scared to move. Then his hand closed around the amulet and he felt suddenly brave. He took one step, then another, and found himself inside the lair.

All at once sweat began pouring from his face. The cave was damp and hot, steaming hot! The horrible odor of the great beast filled the wet air. Galen held fast to his amulet and hurled his challenge.

"Vermithrax!" he cried aloud.

The name of the dragon echoed down the long, winding corridors of the cave. Then the sound ended, in a heavy, deadly silence. Hot as it was inside the cave, Galen felt a slow chill creeping up his spine.

All at once, he heard a sound like distant thunder coming from below his feet. Now the roar rose up to surround him. Louder and louder it grew. The cave trembled. The rocky roof above creaked and sagged. Small pieces of rock broke away to shower down around him. Galen wanted to run back. But he held fast. "My master's work be done," he told himself, and kept on going.

But now, from the darkest depths of the cavern, thick black smoke came pouring. It blew against Galen's body and curled around him like a foul-smelling snake. He could not breathe. He could not see. Choking, he turned and fled, only to fall blindly against the burning hot walls. At last, he reached the entrance of the cave and stumbled out of it, fighting for air.

Valerian broke away from the others and rushed up to him. "Tell me something," she demanded. "What is so wonderful about risking your life?"

"Nothing!" Galen gasped. "Absolutely nothing. You're right. I'll find another way." Stepping back, he began to study the mountain.

A gigantic boulder up above the entrance to the lair caught his eye. Gazing at it steadily, Galen pressed the amulet in his hand, and cast his spell.

"Rock that sits on high hilltop,
Upon thyself, I bid thee drop.
If thou will rid thyself of cave,
And make this dragon's home his grave,
Then I shall make thee always green,
Trees shall grow and birds be seen.
In all the earth there shall not be,
As loved a mountainside as thee!"

A great silence fell everywhere around the young sorcerer. The air was so still that the cave's mouth stopped smoking.

And then it happened. The boulder shook itself loose, tipped over, and began to hurtle down the long, steep mountainside. As it fell, it gathered force, crashing into the rocks below it. These too broke away, smashing into still other rocks.

It was true that Galen had hoped to block off the lair. But he had not understood the full power of the amulet. For this was a land-slide! As Galen and the others ran for cover, half of the vast mountain split off and came roaring down upon itself. On and on came the thundering boulders, as if the earth itself was turning inside out.

It was a long time before Galen and the Urlanders felt safe enough to come out of their hiding places. When they did, they saw that nothing was the same. The cave of the mighty dragon had been crushed beneath ten thousand tons of solid rock. The dragon's lair was no more!

When the travelers brought the news to their village, there was great rejoicing. People danced and sang and clapped each other on the back. Galen was a hero! The children of the town followed him everywhere, begging him to perform wonders.

That evening, for the first time in her life, Valerian put aside the clothes of a man. Dressed as a maiden in a frock of blue, she left her house and went out into the crowd.

"What is this?" exclaimed the

villagers. "Valerian a woman? And we never knew it!"

They stared so hard at her that she wanted to run away. But Galen stretched out his arm to the shy and lovely maiden. Softly, her hand glided into his, and he led her to the dance.

Long into the night, the merry-making continued. Night ended, day came, then night returned once more. Still the people laughed and sang and filled their mugs with golden ale. But all the good cheer ended when Tyrian and his horsemen came galloping into the village square.

"The king has heard of your great deed!" Tyrian called to Galen. "He wants to reward you!" He drew closer to Galen. "Sorcerer! By the king's command, you must come with me now!"

Galen knew better than to trust the knight. But he could not refuse an order of the king. Besides, he thought, the amulet will keep me safe. And so he left the village and rode with Tyrian to the royal castle.

As soon as they arrived, Galen was taken to the throne room. I wonder what the king will offer me as a reward, thought Galen. The hand of his daughter in marriage? A chest of jewels? A pot of gold?

But the king offered him nothing. Not even a smile. Instead, he looked coldly at Galen and said in an icy voice, "You must tell me how you destroyed the dragon."

"Well, sire," Galen began. "I decided that the best way to—"

"One moment," said the king.

"If you don't step closer, I won't hear every word."

Galen moved nearer to the throne and began again. "I decided that —"

"No, no. Closer still, if you please," interrupted the king. "For I must confess that I am hard of hearing."

The king's daughter, Elspeth, looked strangely at her father. But Galen stepped right up to the foot of the throne.

Quick as a cat, the king lunged forward and grabbed hold of the amulet. "*Here* is your magic!" he cried. "In *this!*" He tore it from Galen's neck and snapped, "You broke my pact with the dragon. For that you shall pay!"

Without the magic power of the amulet, Galen could not put up a fight against the king's men. And so it was that he found himself thrown head first into a dungeon cell deep below the castle.

What am I going to do now? Galen wondered. Without the amulet I am powerless. Tyrian will surely have me killed. He sighed heavily. Suddenly he heard a woman's voice calling softly, "Sorcerer?" He ran to the barred iron door and beheld the princess Elspeth.

"Be of hope," she said. "I will help you. I shall speak to my father. I know he will forgive you."

"But for what?" Galen asked. "I killed the dragon!"

"Yes, but suppose you had failed, and it had lived. Would it not have grown angry? Would it not have come out of its lair and sought revenge upon the kingdom?"

"I knew I could kill it," said Galen. "And it had to die! How else could the lotteries and the terrible sacrifices of young maidens be stopped?"

"The lotteries protected us," replied Elspeth. "That is why my father started them. Choosing one out of many to die kept the rest of us from harm. I would have gone to my death happily if my name had been chosen," she declared.

"Ah, Princess," said Galen. "You have been kept from the truth. All the world knows that your name never went into the box of chance."

"How can you say that?" cried the princess. "You lie! You *lie!!!*"

Before Galen could reply, the princess had run out of the dungeon.

The king was in his library when Elspeth rushed in. "Father!" she cried. "I must speak to you!"

"Not now, child," he said, rubbing the amulet. "I am turning lead to gold—if I can just get the hang of it!"

But the princess would not wait. "Answer me truly," she demanded. "Have you shamed me before all the people of this land?"

"What a question you ask, child," said the king softly. "Why speak you so?"

"Is it true that I did not risk my life with the other maidens?"

"Who says such a thing? I shall have him beheaded!"

"Father, answer me!"

"Child! Your name went in with all the rest."

"On the king's honor?"

"Aye!" said the king. "On the king's honor." But he could not look at her as he said it.

Then Elspeth knew that he was lying. "Oh, Father," she whispered, "what have you done to me?" Turning quickly, she ran from the room.

"Elspeth, wait!" The king started after her. But suddenly he fell to the floor, as the whole castle began to shake.

That moment, all over the kingdom, the earth was groaning and heaving. Trees broke away from their roots and crashed to the ground. Houses shook until their roofs fell in. Birds and animals fled in all directions. The people, too, ran from their homes to open places. Trembling with fear, they clung to one another. They all knew what was causing the disaster. It was the beast! The dragon was alive! It was pushing its way out of the fallen mountain!

Down in the castle dungeon, Galen realized what had happened. "I've failed!" he cried. "The dragon will destroy the kingdom — and it's all my fault! I must get out! I must get out!" He pulled at the door with all the strength in his body. But it would not budge. He tried again and again. It was no use. Then suddenly, as if by magic, it flew open.

As he raced out, Galen thought he saw the princess in the dungeon hall. Had she freed him? He wasn't sure. But there was no time to waste.

I must get out of the castle, he thought, leaping up the stairs three at a time. I'll find a horse and . . . Then he saw a door. But Tyrian himself stood in the way. Galen turned and ran, and the knight came after him, sword in hand.

The castle shook again, even harder than before. In the courtyard outside, the soldiers' horses went mad with fright. Tyrian ran to a window. "Close the main gate before we lose the horses!" he shouted to his men.

This was Galen's chance. With lightning speed, he sprang past Tyrian out of the castle and onto a fleeing horse.

"Stop him!" screamed the knight.

Horse and rider raced for the gate. Seconds before they reached it, the gate slammed shut. Galen looked desperately for a way out, as a crowd of Tyrian's soldiers closed in on him. He realized there was only one thing he could do. Turning his horse around, he rode straight at his attackers. They leaped aside, and Galen and his horse galloped up the steps and into the castle!

Up and down the halls of the shaking castle he rode. Everywhere he turned there were armed men coming at him. At last, he burst into the royal library.

"Ye gods!" cried the king, falling back. "Help! Save me!"

Tyrian rushed in with a group of his men. Galen was trapped. His back was to the wall. The soldiers closed in for the kill. But then the wall itself collapsed from the force of the quake. Horse and rider leaped through the hole!

Once outside, they headed for the gate. Would it trap them again? No! For the quake had thrown it to the ground. Free at last, Galen spurred his horse to a gallop and headed for the village.

It was night when Galen approached the village. As he drew closer, he heard screams and cries, and saw fires raging everywhere. Oh no! he thought. Vermithrax has attacked!

Suddenly Galen heard a loud flapping sound and felt a rush of hot, foul air. He gazed up. There, over his head, was the monstrous black shape of the dragon. Its sharp claws were like gleaming curved knives. Jets of fire burst from its huge jagged mouth. Its eyes were cold and yellow.

As Galen watched in horror, the beast swooped down over a row of houses and blasted them with flame. They went up like giant torches. With a shriek of rage, the beast lifted up into the sky and flew away.

Sick at heart, Galen rode into the village. He jumped down from his horse and began helping some villagers put out a fire.

"Sorcerer!" screamed an old woman when she saw him. "This is your fault!"

Others stopped their work. They glared at Galen. When he saw the rage in their faces, he thought, they blame me. And they are right! But I never thought it could come to this!

A mob was forming. "Let's get him!" someone shouted. Galen started to run. The mob gave chase. Turning quickly into an alley, Galen lost them. Then he saw Valerian up ahead. She was standing in front of a house that had lost its roof.

He called to her, but she turned away and went inside. Galen looked around. The mob was after him again, throwing sticks and rocks.

Racing across the alley, he burst into Valerian's house and slammed the door behind him.

"What a mess you have made!" Valerian said to him angrily. "You and your magic!" She picked up a pitchfork and pointed it at him. "Get out of this house!"

Galen was so unhappy he could not speak. It would not have mattered if she *had* stuck him with the pitchfork. He almost wished she would. He felt that he deserved it.

The sight of Galen's pitiful face was too much for Valerian. She sighed, shook her head, and slowly laid down the pitchfork.

"The king's men will be coming after me soon," said Galen.

And he was right. The very next day, Tyrian and his men pushed their way into the house. "Search every hiding place!" the knight commanded.

"Who are you looking for?" asked Valerian innocently.

"You know very well," snapped Tyrian.

"There's a blacksmith shop through there!" one of the men reported. "It belongs to her father."

Tyrian rushed into the shop. There stood Simon, Valerian's father, working away at his anvil.

"May I help you, sir?" asked Simon with a pleasant smile. "If your horse needs shoes, you've come to the right place."

The knight glared at Simon. "I see that the magician has turned your son into a daughter," he sneered. "But he chose the wrong time to do it. Now her name can go into the box of chance with all the others."

The smile froze on Simon's face. "B-but the sacrifice was only a few days ago!"

"That was before the dragon grew angry," shouted the knight as he left. "Now there must be another! Soon!"

When the soldiers were gone, Valerian moved her father's anvil. Galen crawled out of the hiding place underneath and heaved a sigh of relief. "I will need a weapon to slay the dragon," he told Simon.

"Are you mad?" Valerian shouted.

"Well, if I can't be a magician," said Galen, "I'll be a madman. I might do better at it."

"You are welcome to any of the swords and lances in the shop," said Simon. "I made them all myself. They're all good."

"Blacksmith," said Galen, "no ordinary weapon will cut into the beast." He looked Simon in the eye. "Give me your secret one. The one you have been hiding."

"By my beard!" exclaimed Simon. "How came you to know that? I told no one of it. Not even Valerian!"

"Even a fool like myself can sometimes guess what a wise man is up to," said Galen. "You have been clever enough to save Valerian from the game of chance all these years. You must have been thinking about a way to get rid of the threat altogether."

"Wait right here!" cried the smith. He returned a moment later with a long, gleaming lance. It was beautiful and strong—powerful enough to cut through solid iron. "I made it years ago," he said. "And I have waited all this time for a warrior to come. Alas, I am not one myself."

"Well, neither is he!" cried Valerian. She turned to Galen. "Forget about it. You can't do it."

"I *am* going to need a little help," Galen replied, thinking of the amulet. "I must find a way to get into the castle."

The next night, by royal command, all the maidens of the kingdom gathered together for the lottery. They stood before the castle in a frightened group, looking at the dreaded box of chance that held their names.

Standing with them, Valerian was overcome with fear. Her days of outwitting the terrible choosing were over, and she was certain that her name would be drawn. Now she waited with a pounding heart for the ritual to begin.

Near the maidens stood a crowd of parents, relatives, and friends. They too waited fearfully for the king and his men to appear. Galen, dressed as a farm boy, went unnoticed. Keeping his face hidden under a wide-brimmed hat, he stood at the edge of the crowd, watching the castle.

At last, the trumpets sounded to announce the coming of the king. Slowly, he walked onto the platform with the princess. Then he signaled for the lottery to begin. The king's herald, a man named Horsrik, walked slowly to the box of chance. He poured the wooden tiles bearing the maidens' names into a large barrel.

"Stir the tiles!" shouted the people. Horsrik stirred them with a long stick until they were well mixed.

"Draw the name!" cried the crowd. Horsrik reached slowly into the barrel and brought out a single wooden tile. No one dared to breathe. Parents and maidens bit their lips. Hearts stood still.

But what was this? Why was Horsrik so silent? Why didn't he call out the name? The people waited until they could stand it no longer. "The name! The name!" they cried. But still Horsrik said nothing.

"Read the name!" ordered the king.

Horsrik could not disobey a royal command. But he trembled as he said, "It is Princess El—"

"Hold!" screamed the king.

"You have made a mistake!" He tore the wooden piece out of the herald's hands and stared at it.

"I cannot read this name," he cried. "The writing is unclear. Let another tile be drawn!" He pushed aside the shaking herald and went to the barrel himself. "I will do it," he said.

The king thrust his hand deep down among the pieces and drew a tile. He started to read the name on it aloud, but stopped suddenly. The people stared at each other and began to whisper. Their excitement grew. The king's soldiers smelled trouble. By silent agreement, their hands went to the hilts of their swords.

"Read out the name! Tell us the name!" shouted the crowd impa-tiently. But the king remained speechless.

The princess stood up. "The name," she cried, "is my own. Princess Elspeth of Urland!"

The king's eyes grew wild. He reached into the barrel with both hands and pulled out tile after tile. "They're all the same!" he screamed, flinging them into the crowd. "Look! Look! See for your-selves! This drawing is false! It does not count! Her name is on them all!"

"It *does* count!" cried Elspeth. "Because in the past my name was *never* on the tiles." Her voice grew softer as she turned to the king. "It has to be this way, Father, don't you see? Now I shall have my honor back."

At this moment, the eyes of everyone in the crowd were fixed upon the unhappy king and his daughter. All eyes, that is, except Galen's. He knew that this was his chance to slip unseen into the castle. And he made the most of it.

Hurrying inside, he wondered where to start his search for the amulet. He decided on the throne room, and looked around it quickly. No amulet. Then he tried the counting room, where the king kept his treasures. Still no luck. Moving swiftly down the hallway, he saw that the door to the library was open. In he went.

He was going through a stack of books and boxes when he heard footsteps behind him. Whirling around, he was met by the stern faces of the king and Tyrian. Galen sprang desperately for the window, but Tyrian was there ahead of him, pointing a sword at his heart.

"Stop!" commanded the king. "Put up thy blade! Do not harm him!"

Scowling, Tyrian obeyed. He wanted more than anything to get rid of Galen for good. The king was wrong not to allow it, he thought. He was becoming weak. Undone—just because of a silly girl! Didn't he realize that his kingdom was in danger? That the people would rise up if Elspeth was not given to the dragon?

But the king did not care what Tyrian—or anyone—thought. He wanted only to save the princess. He smiled weakly at Galen. "Do you want your amulet?" he asked. "Here it is." The king removed it from around his neck and handed it to the young sorcerer. "I don't know how to use this thing very well," he said. "But I'm sure that if you tried again with it, very hard—"

"Sire!" cried Tyrian. "Do not send him against the dragon. The beast will destroy the kingdom!"

But the king would not listen to the knight's warning. "Save my child," he pleaded with Galen. "Save her, I beg of you!"

Back in the village at Simon's blacksmith shop, Galen held the amulet above the lance and spoke:

"Mighty weapon,
Hark to me!
Thou shall set a people free!
If this task be truly thine,
Let me see thy spirit shine!"

The lance began to glow from within with a pure, bright fire. The blacksmith and Galen smiled at each other. "An edge like no other on this earth!" said Simon. "It will surely slay the dragon!"

Valerian was not so sure. No one had yet lived through a blast of dragon flame. So she left the village and journeyed by herself to the lair in search of dragon scales. There she found many, scattered among the bones of past victims. But the best and the biggest were at the very mouth of the cave. As she stooped to pick them up, two small scaly creatures leaped out at her. Baby dragons! Valerian's heart pounded. The dragons hissed at her. One of them snapped at her boot with its sharp teeth. She kicked it away, turned, and ran.

On his way up the mountainside, Galen met Valerian. She warned him about the baby dragons. And she presented him with a gift. It was a fire shield, made from the scales that protected the dragon's own body. She hoped it would protect Galen. She had risked her own life because she had secretly begun to fall in love with the young sorcerer.

Galen took the shield gratefully. Then he kissed Valerian good-bye and went forth to seek the dragon.

When he arrived at the dragon's lair, Galen saw that there were soldiers near the mouth of the cave. They were tying Princess Elspeth to a wooden post. Beside her stood the herald, Horsrik, reading aloud.

"Oh, noble dragon!" he cried. "See how we love thee. For here is the daughter of our king! Take her and enjoy your feast! And may you—"

Suddenly, the long scroll in the herald's hands burst into flames, and Galen appeared in a puff of smoke. Frightened by this show of magic, Horsrik turned and ran. So did all the soldiers, except one.

"Sword against lance!" cried Tyrian, as he leaped at Galen. His sword lunged for the lad's heart. Galen's lance caught the blow. Tyrian thrust again. Though Galen knew nothing about dueling, he trusted the power of the lance. Again and again the long weapon fended off the furious attacks of the knight.

Tyrian was an evil man, but a great fighter. Slowly, slowly, he drove Galen up the mountain. As Galen retreated, his foot caught in an opening between the rocks—and down he went!

Tyrian was sure that he had won at last. He was rushing in for the kill, when the ground shuddered. The knight staggered, giving Galen a chance to scramble to his feet. Then the ground shook again, and both men were thrown against the rocks.

"Run, the two of you! Run for your lives!" the princess screamed. "The beast comes forth!"

Galen ran to the princess. With one slash of his lance, he split the

chains that held her prisoner. But now Tyrian leaped back into the fight. As sword and lance clashed, the princess walked directly into the smoking cave.

"No! No!" cried Galen.

Catching the youth off guard, Tyrian lashed out with his weapon. But Galen saw the blow coming out of the corner of his eye and darted behind the wooden post. Tyrian's blade just missed him and hit the post instead.

"Now!" cried Galen to his lance as he drove it right into the post. The sharp point cut through the thick wood as if it were butter. Straight through went the point, and out the other side, plunging directly into Tyrian's heart! A look of amazement spread over the knight's face. It froze there forever, as he fell back dead.

Pulling his weapon free, Galen raced into the cave calling Elspeth's name. But there was no answer. He rushed on, hoping to find her before it was too late.

Suddenly he stopped. There, at the end of the tunnel, were three red-eyed baby dragons. They were busily feeding on a corpse—the body of Princess Elspeth.

The sight made Galen sick. "No!" he cried. "Stop!"

The baby dragons did not like this interruption. Hissing, they bared their sharp claws and turned on Galen.

Galen raised his lance. All his fear was gone. In its place was a terrible anger at the princess's death. He slew the baby dragons one by one, and continued down the tunnel. He was ready to attack Vermithrax now, if it meant going down into the burning core of the earth!

Soon it seemed as if that was just where he was headed. The farther down he went, the hotter the walls grew. Glowing drops of water fell from above and sizzled on the ground. He grew dizzy with the heat, but stumbled on.

At last, he burst out of the cave into another world—an underground world! A vast lake spread out before him. Waves of fire swept over its boiling surface. The only path ahead was a line of flat rocks jutting out of the burning water. Now there was no turning back. Galen stepped out onto the rocks.

They were very slippery. One wrong step and he would go toppling into the flames. Carefully, he moved from rock to rock. All the while, his eyes searched the lake, but there was no sign of the dragon. Yet Galen had the awful feeling that he was being watched— that somewhere in the lake of fire, the serpent was lying in wait for him, drawing him ever farther out to meet his doom.

All at once the waters flew apart and the huge head of Vermithrax shot to the surface. The long scaly neck rose high up out of the water like a living mountain. A smell so poisonous that it made Galen's head swim filled the air. The monster's cold, yellow, unblinking eyes gazed down, fixing Galen in their icy glare. The lad told himself to run. To defend himself. To do *something!* But he couldn't move. He was frozen with terror.

Then Vermithrax roared and spat fire. Just in time, Galen raised his shield against the flames. The beast took a breath, and Galen sprang across the rocks, running for his life.

As he got to the tunnel, a wave of dragon fire singed the hair on the back of Galen's head. He ran even faster. Soon he reached the place where the baby dragons lay. With the sound of the beast roaring after him, Galen flung himself into a hollow in the tunnel wall. Then he waited.

Just as Galen had hoped, when the dragon appeared, it stopped to examine its dead children. This

was Galen's chance. He leaped out of the hiding place and plunged the lance deep into the brown, leathery neck of the huge beast.

With a fearful howl, the monster threw itself against the walls of the cave. Galen's lance was magically sharp, but it had an ordinary wooden shaft. Now the shaft snapped against a wall and the wall itself began to crack. The mountain shook with the dragon's fury. Vermithrax reared and let loose another blast of flame. Gal-en covered himself with the shield and dropped to the ground. Fire swirled around him.

Was it luck? Was it the power of the amulet? Galen would never know. But when the quake was over, the young sorcerer lay just barely alive on the ground outside the lair. It was Valerian who found him, and brought him home. There, she tended his wounds with loving care.

While Galen was getting better, he had the time to think about all that had happened. He thought about Ulrich and old Hodge. About the dragon and the lake of fire in its lair.

LAKE OF FIRE?! Suddenly Galen remembered the little pouch of Ulrich's ashes, and Hodge's dying words: "Throw them in the lake of fire. . . . Burning water! . . . Find it."

"Why, that old magical trickster!" shouted Galen. "Ulrich planned it all! He knew everything from the start!"

Grabbing the bag of ashes, Galen raced off once more for the dragon's lair. Valerian chased after him, pleading with him to stop. But he would not.

"Very well, then," she said. "I'm going with you!"

Galen could not talk her out of it, and they entered the cave together. Once inside, he managed to slip away from her. At first Valerian looked for him, but then she gave up, and headed back outside.

Leaving the cave, Valerian was amazed to see that the sky was dark. But how could that be? It was daytime!

Then she saw a strange and wonderful thing happening in the sky. The rising moon had crossed the path of the sun. Like a hand that passes in front of a light, it was blocking the sun's rays. In the middle of the day, the darkness of deepest night descended upon the land.

The sight of this filled Valerian with such awe that she did not hear the flapping sound of great leathery wings as they approached. Nor did she see the serpent landing near her in the darkness. Only

when the dark head of the monster blotted out what was left of the sun and moon did she realize what was standing over her. VERMITHRAX!

She turned and ran. A huge winged claw came down and cut off her escape. She ran the other way. Another claw came down in front of her. She was trapped!

Meanwhile, hurrying along inside the cave, Galen had reached the lake of fire. He opened the bag and cast Ulrich's ashes into the lake, crying,

> *"Powers of Earth*
> *And burning Sun,*
> *Now let my master's*
> *Will be done!"*

The flames on the water slowly gathered themselves into a circle and began to turn. Slowly at first, then faster and faster they whirled. Then, lo and behold! A vision formed in the swirling flames. It was in the shape of a man. But *this* man was more than a vision. As Galen watched, he rose up and stepped out of the fire.

"Master!" shouted Galen, overcome with joy. "You're alive!!!"

"That is a surprise to you, but not to me," said Ulrich quietly. "Let us go now, lad, and quickly.

> *For the Moon lies now*
> *Before the Sun.*
> *This is the time*
> *When deeds are done!"*

Outside, the serpent had grown tired of toying with Valerian. Now it was ready for the kill. Its hideous jaws opened wide . . .

"Vermithrax!" cried a man's voice. "Hail to thee, my enemy of old!"

The dragon looked around and saw the wizard emerging from the lair. It blinked, as if in surprise.

Ulrich stepped closer to the serpent. "You are old," he said, "and so am I. The world has seen enough of sorcerers, and certainly enough of dragons. Your day is done. Begone!"

Feeling some power greater than its own, the dragon lifted its great wings and rose into the air. Valerian and Galen rushed into each other's arms. The old man smiled, but his mind was on the battle that lay ahead.

"Lad, hear my words," he said to Galen. "You brought me from the flames. Now you must send me back. You must destroy the amulet and myself along with it."

"What??" said Galen. "But I can't!"

"You will know the moment," said the old wizard. He raised his staff and vanished abruptly in a green flash. An instant later he appeared upon a high rocky place. At that moment the moon slid over the last arc of the sun and the sky grew dark. Then the white

flare of the sun's corona shone forth in all its glory. The dragon, perched upon another mountaintop, stirred uneasily and took flight again.

"Make haste!" Galen shouted to Valerian. "We must help him."

As they scrambled up the mountainside, they heard a cry that made their blood freeze. From out of the sky swooped the shrieking dragon, hurling fire from its mouth. But the wizard caused great storm clouds to roll out over the land. Now lightning shot forth at the sorcerer's command. Fire and thunderbolt met head-on, and the dragon was wounded. Screaming in pain, it veered off into the distance and was lost from sight.

The old man stood alone on the rock waiting for the dragon's next attack. The wind blew around the mountain, carrying the sound of flapping wings. Then, all at once, the serpent came hurtling down on Ulrich from behind! Flames leaped from its mouth straight at the wizard. Quickly, Ulrich lifted his magic staff and beat them off. But the dragon kept coming. A jagged claw ripped at the magician's arm as the beast flew past.

Hurt and bleeding, the old man staggered. The dragon, smelling blood, circled in the air and prepared to attack again.

"Quick!" exclaimed Valerian. "Smash the amulet!"

"No! I can't kill him! I can't!" cried Galen.

Valerian lunged for the amulet. It fell to the ground. As she and Galen struggled over it, a great silence fell over the mountains. They looked up. Ulrich stood on the mountaintop with his arms spread and his eyes closed. He looked strangely calm. Was he

giving up, or about to play a final trick?

Down, down, the flying monster swooped, until its horrible claws reached out for the old man—and carried him off into the sky!

"Galen! Galen!" the wizard cried out, twisting in the dragon's terrible grasp.

The young man's eyes filled with tears and his hands shook. But he knew that the time had come. He must act—now. Raising a rock high above his head, he smashed the amulet with all his might. It broke into a thousand pieces. And as it did, the sky exploded. It was the dragon bursting apart! For a moment the air was filled with death—and then it was over. The great beast and the great sorcerer were gone forever.

And so the people of Urland were free of the terrible dragon at last. No more would their daughters be sacrificed. No more would they fear the raging anger of the beast.

"No more," said Valerian, happily, "will I have to worry about you trying to be a sorcerer."

"I feel the same way you do," said Galen, as the two of them walked hand in hand through a meadow.

"If you had the amulet, you'd be getting into all kinds of trouble with it," she said.

"You're absolutely right," he agreed. "I just wish . . ."

"Yes?"

They had been walking for hours and were both getting tired. ". . . well, that we had a horse," he said with a sigh.

A moment later, they heard a horse's cry. A beautiful white stallion came galloping out of the woods to lay its soft face against Valerian's cheek.

"What is this?" she asked.

"Probably a horse," said Galen, as surprised as Valerian.

"Did you . . . ?" She gave him a very strange look.

"How could I? It must have been wandering loose. Or wild."

Galen mounted the beautiful animal and reached down for Valerian.

"Wait!" she said. "You just wished for a horse and here it is."

"Shall I wish it away?"

Valerian thought this over. No, better not. Up she went to join Galen on the horse. And together they rode away.